Everybody's Favorite Series No. 8

&

Strauss Waltz Album

FOREWORD The origin of the waltz has been the subject of much controversy. There is, however, little doubt but that it was an adaptation of the "Ländler," a dance indulged in extensively by the peasants of Southern Germany.

Mozart, Beethoven, Schubert and Weber—each in his turn, contributed much in developing the Waltz.

In France, the Waltz made its appearance between 1792 and 1801, and a few days later was introduced in England. Here it was greeted with a storm of criticism, but in spite of its initial reception, achieved rapid popularity.

In the early part of the ninetenth century, the composition of Waltzes for dancing was almost entirely in the hands of Viennese writers, and it was Johann Strauss the elder, who introduced the style of naming them. In Vienna, under the Strauss family, the Waltz became fixed in the form in which we know it, i.e. an introduction, generally in slow tempo and foreshadowing the principal motive of the composition, followed by five or six separate waltzes, and ending with a Coda recapitulating the principal themes.

Johann Strauss II was born in Vienna, October 25, 1825. He studied music against the wishes of his father and later conducted his orchestra in all the principal cities of Europe, including St. Petersburg, where he was received magnificently. He conducted too, at the brilliant Court Balls in Vienna. In addition to his famous Waltz compositions, he wrote several charming operettas among which were "The Bat" and "The Gypsy Baron." Richard Wagner, commenting on his compositions, said in part . . . "They far surpass in charm, finish and real musical worth, hundreds of artificial compositions of his contemporaries." Strauss died in 1899.

THE PUBLISHER

© Copyright 1934
Amsco Music Publishing Company
240 West 55th Street, New York 19, New York
International Copyright Secured
All Rights Reserved

Contents

The Beautiful Blue Danube
(An der schonen blauen Donau)

INTRO.

JOHANN STRAUSS, Op. 314

Andantino

Tempo di Valse

WALTZ

1.

5

6

5.

Vienna Life
(Wiener Blut)

JOHANN STRAUSS, Op. 354

INTRO.
Allegro moderato

Andante

Tempo di Valse

WALTZ

1.

Ped. simile

Ped. simile

mf

sempre cresc.

Ped. simile

Ending

Fine

Dal Segno al Fine

16

Wine, Woman and Song
(Wein, Weib und Gesang)

JOHANN STRAUSS, Op. 333

INTRO.
Andantino

Allegro moderato

Ped. simile

senza pedale

WALTZ

1.

24

INTRO. WALTZ

3.

CODA

Kiss-Waltz
(Kuss-Walzer)

INTRO.
Andantino maestoso

JOHANN STRAUSS, Op. 400

29

Ped.simile

mf

fz

p

f

p poco rit.

p

f

f

Waltz D.C. al ⊕

Artist's Life
(Künstler-Leben)

INTRO.
Andante moderato

cantabile

JOHANN STRAUSS, Op. 316

Tempo di Valse

WALTZ

37

Tales from the Vienna Woods
(Geschichten aus dem Wiener-Wald)

INTRO.
Tempo di Valse

JOHANN STRAUSS Op 325

44

Vivace

Tempo I

Tempo di Valse

WALTZ

1.

Ped. simile

46

49

Southern Roses
(Rosen aus dem Süden)

INTRO.
Andantino

JOHANN STRAUSS, Op. 388

54

55

58

senza Ped.

Ped. simile

To Alfred Grünfeld

Voices of Spring
(Frühlingsstimmen)

JOHANN STRAUSS, Op. 410

Tempo di Valse

65

66

Du und Du

Waltzes from "Fledermaus" (The "Bat")

JOHANN STRAUSS, Op. 367

WALTZ

1.

Fine

D. S. al Fine

72

D. S. al Fine 𝄋

INTRO.

WALTZ

3.

CODA

Thousand and One Nights
(Tausend und eine Nacht)

JOHANN STRAUSS, Op. 346

INTRO.
Andante

Tempo di Valse

WALTZ

1.

TRIO

3.

Kaiser Waltz

JOHANN STRAUSS, Op. 437

INTRO.
Slow march tempo

1.

91

4.

ff marc. molto

Ped. simile

Skip(ad lib.) from here to sign ⊕

O Beautiful May

JOHANN STRAUSS, Op. 375

1.

D. S. al Fine

Tempo di Valse

Morning Journals

JOHANN STRAUSS, Op. 279

109

D.C. al Fine

Ped. simile

2.

Fine

D.S. al Fine

3.

Fine

D.S. al Fine

5.

D.S. al Fine

CODA

Treasure Waltz

From the "Gypsy Baron"

JOHANN STRAUSS, Op. 418

120

122

D.S. al Fine

Viennese Melody

Andantino

Waltz in A Flat

JOHANNES BRAHMS, Op 39, No. 15
(1833-1897)

Teneramente e grazioso (♩ = 116)

Waves of the Danube
(Donauwellen)

J. IVANOVICI

INTRO.
Allegro moderato

Andante

WALTZ

1.

FINALE

Waltz
from
"Faust"

C. GOUNOD

Tempo di Valse

Love's Dream after the Ball
(Songe d'amour après le bal)

ALPHONSE CZIBULKA, Op. 356

Tempo di Valse

Andante con amore

cresc. e string.

con espressione e rit. assai

decresc.

pp

morendo

Tempo di Valse

pp

poco rit.

a tempo, ma un pochettino più lento

ppp

Ped. simile

Come To The Sea!
(Vieni Sul Mar)

Venetian Melody

INTRO.
Tempo di Valse

Valse

Il Bacio Waltz
(The Kiss)

L. ARDITI

Over The Waves
(Sobre las Olas)

JUVENTINO ROSAS

Valse

154

Vilia

FRANZ LEHAR

Tempo di Valse

Merry Widow Waltz

F. LEHÁR

Tempo di Valse *Molto e tranquillo*

D.C.

The Skaters

EMIL WALDTEUFEL, Op. 183

INTRO.
Andante

D.S.

CODA

Risoluto 𝄋

2.

Schellen (*Grelots*)

D.S.

CODA

3.

p espressivo

Ped. simile

Grazioso

168

4.

D.C. al Fin

Ped. simile

Estudiantina
Suite de Valses

ÉMILE WALDTEUFEL, Op. 191

INTRO.
Tempo di Valse

Valse
ESTUDIANTINA *(REFRAIN)*

1.

ESTUDIANTINA *(COUPLET)*

2.

CHANSON D' AUTOMNE

JOTA DE LA ESTUDIANTINA

3.

TIRANA

Ped. simile

Fine

D.S.

DE CADIZ AL PUERTO

EL TRIPILI

CODA

Dolorès
VALSE

EMILE WALDTEUFEL, Op. 170

INTRO.
Maestoso energico

Doloroso

1.

182

Waltz Serenade

From "Les Millions d'Arlequin"

RICHARD DRIGO

Tempo di Valse

A Waltz Dream

OSCAR STRAUSS

Come Back To Sorrento!

E. DE CURTIS